Good Habits for God's Kids

Good for You

WRITTEN BY LAURA DERICO

ILLUSTRATED BY ANGELA KAMSTRA

09 08 07 06 05 04   9 8 7 6 5 4 3 2

Standard
PUBLISHING
CINCINNATI, OHIO

"Broccoli? Green beans? Brussels sprouts?!? DAD?!?" Oscar shouted.

"Where is all the *good* food?" he asked, peering into the refrigerator.

"This food *is* good, Oscar—it's good for you! God gave us healthy bodies, and we need to take better care of them by eating healthy foods and exercising," Dad said.

"Maybe it's good for *you*, but I don't need that stuff—I'm young! Besides, eating green things all the time and doing chin-ups is boring," Oscar whined.

"OK, Oscar, for the next week, you can eat what you want and not exercise. What do you say?" Oscar's dad asked.

"I say that's great! Wait till my friends find out!" Oscar said happily.

When Howard and Sara Beth came over later, they were thrilled to see the table full of all their favorite goodies. The three friends stuffed their mouths with Cheesy Fluff, Sugar Sticks, and Coco-Chews. They slurped up soda pop and chomped up chips.

They slouched on the couch, flopped on the floor, and became blobs on the beanbag chairs. They ate so much they couldn't even move!

After five video games and three bags of snacks, it was time for Howard and Sara Beth to go home. "Wow, Oscar, that was yummy, but I sure do feel funny," said Howard, rubbing his tummy.

"Yawwwnnn! I'm so sleepy! If I ate like that every day, I'd never make it through the church picnic race next month," Sara Beth said.

"Well, I love to eat whatever I want. I know I'll make it through that race—I might even win!" Oscar replied.

The next morning, Oscar slept late and skipped breakfast. When he finally got up, Dad was already dressed in his jogging clothes. "Would you like to exercise with me today, Oscar?" Dad asked.

"No way!" Oscar said. "I don't need any exercise. Besides, I'm going to Sara Beth's house today."

Oscar had fun with Sara Beth and his other friends all afternoon until they decided to run relay races. Oscar ran as fast as he could, but he lost every time. Even little Simon, who was only four, beat him. So Oscar trudged home and had cold pizza and ice cream for dinner

The next day, Oscar had a big bowl of Sugar Poofs for breakfast. "Sure you don't want to exercise with me today?" Dad asked.

Oscar said, "No way! I don't need any exercise. I'm going to play at Howard's house."

At Howard's house, everybody swam laps in the pool to see who could do the most in five minutes. Oscar paddled and splashed, but he could only do one lap. Even little Simon did three! Oscar sloshed home and ate another bowl of Sugar Poofs.

The next day, Oscar and his dad walked to meet Oscar's friends at the bottom of Big Hill. "So no exercise again today, Oscar?" Dad asked.

"No way, Dad! I told you I don't need that stuff. I'm just going to play with my friends," Oscar grumped. His head hurt and he felt very grouchy. Oscar ate a candy bar as he waited for his friends.

All the friends climbed up Big Hill, but Oscar didn't even get halfway up before he had to rest. He huffed, puffed, and plopped down on the ground. Then he watched as all of his friends—even that little Simon!—cheered as they reached the top. Oscar just sighed, stumbled back down the hill, and shuffled home.

Oscar was thirsty and hungry, but none of his soda or snacks looked good. "What's wrong, Oscar?" Dad asked.

"Dad, I'm a loser! I'm so slow, and I get so tired. Even Simon is faster than me! I'll never win that church race now," Oscar said, slumping on the couch.

"Oscar, you're no loser. God designed our bodies, and he's also provided the food to help them do what they need to do. But there is something we need to do, too," Dad said.

"You mean start eating green things and doing chin-ups?" Oscar asked.

"Not exactly," Dad smiled.

The next day, Oscar's dad made a delicious breakfast. "You mean this is good for me?" Oscar asked.

"Yes, Oscar, green vegetables are good, but there are all kinds of food you can and should eat to keep your body healthy—foods that taste great!" his dad said.

After breakfast, they played soccer in the yard. "You mean, this is exercise?" Oscar asked, bouncing a ball on his knee.

"Yep, that's right," Dad said. "Exercise isn't just doing chin-ups. In fact, you've been exercising all week when you were playing with your friends. But you need to exercise regularly and keep doing activities that will help your muscles stretch and grow—things that you like to do!"

Oscar started doing a little exercise every day. He practiced soccer kicks, skated at the park, and swam laps at the pool. He had fun running races and jumping rope with his pals. Three times a week, Oscar jogged with his dad. Then they raced to see who could do the most sit-ups. Oscar even had fun doing chin-ups!

Oscar's dad also helped him learn how to eat better—and not just green things! They ate balanced meals with good foods full of vitamins and nutrients. Oscar learned to look for healthy food at the grocery, instead of just grabbing stuff full of sugar and fat. Oscar and his dad enjoyed treats every once in a while, but Oscar even started to like the sweet taste of apples and berries better than sugary snacks!

When the Sunday of the race finally arrived, Oscar felt strong, healthy, and very happy! Oscar listened in church as missionaries told about kids in other countries that were sick and had little food.

Oscar prayed, "God, thank you for giving me a healthy body and good food and water every day. Help me to take care of my body and to help others be healthy, too."

Before the race, Oscar made sure to eat an energy-filled lunch and to drink lots of water. Then he joined his friends at the starting line and stretched his arms and legs. They all waited for the signal. BANG! They were off—and Oscar was in the lead!

Oscar's dad waited at the finish line. Several of Oscar's friends finished and waited, too. Where was Oscar?

Finally, Oscar appeared—carrying little Simon on his back! They crossed the finish line and while Oscar caught his breath, Simon explained, "I tripped and hurt my foot, but Oscar helped me. He was able to carry me all the way to the end of the race!"

"Well, son, you may not have won the race, but you sure are a winner. How about we celebrate with some ice cream and strawberries?" Dad said.

"Thanks, Dad, but I'll just take the strawberries," Oscar smiled. "You know, they're good for you!"

Note to Parents

1 Corinthians 6:19 says, "Your body is the temple of the Holy Spirit . . . so you must honor God with your body." This storybook is part of a Happy Day® series designed to help children learn about the good habits of wise living. Use the following suggestions to help your children be responsible to take care of the things God has given them.

Good-For-You Tips

- It's good for kids to be involved in planning and preparing meals. As you work together, teach your child which foods are healthy and which are not.

- If sugary or salty snacks and soda aren't in the house, the kids (and you!) will get used to healthier alternatives. Keep healthy snacks available instead: carrot and celery sticks, grapes, bananas, orange and apple slices, pretzels, and low-salt popcorn.

- Encourage your children to drink milk and lots of water—at least 8 glasses a day.

- Make exercise a fun family event. Play sports, take walks, have family races, or train for a silly family Olympics!

Eat well, have fun, and enjoy the body God gave you!